D0966792

BBC CHILDREN'S BOOKS
Published by the Penguin Group
Penguin Books Ltd, 80 Strand, London WC2R 0RL, England
Penguin Putnam Inc., 375 Hudson Street, New York, New York 10014, USA
Penguin Books Australia Ltd, 250 Camberwell Road, Camberwell, Victoria 3124, Australia
Canada, India, New Zealand, South Africa
First published in 1999 by BBC Worldwide Limited
This edition published by BBC Children's Books, 2005
10 9 8 7 6 5 4 3 2
Text by Diane Redmond
Illustrations by Magic Island
Text, design and illustrations © BBC Children's Books, 2005
The Tweenies name, logo and characters are trademarks of the
British Broadcasting Corporation and are used under licence. © BBC 1998-2001
Tweenies is produced by Tell-Tale Productions for BBC Television
BBC and logo © and ™ BBC 1996. CBeebies and logo ™ BBC. © BBC 2002
ISBN 1 405 90091 1
Printed in China

Looking After Doodles

"Why can't Doodles get his own food?" asked Fizz one day, when she and Bella and Milo and Jake were watching Judy feed the dog.

"Because he can't put food into his own bowl," said Judy. "Somebody has to do it for him. Dogs need looking after."

"Just like children?" asked Milo.

"Looking after a dog isn't the same as looking after children," Judy explained.

"Oh, can we TRY to look after Doodles?" begged Bella. "We can feed him and do things for him. Please?"

"All right," Judy agreed. "I'll be close by if you need any help."

The Tweenies took it in turns to look after Doodles. Fizz went first. She put ribbons in Doodles' hair to make him look pretty.

Then she put a nappy on him!

"Dogs don't wear nappies!" barked Doodles.

"There's nothing to be ashamed of," Fizz insisted. "We've all had to wear them."

When it was Milo's turn to look after Doodles, he fastened a bib around his neck.

"Dogs don't wear bibs!" woofed Doodles.

"You have to keep your fur nice and clean," said Milo. "Now, open wide – dinner time!" and he popped a sandwich into Doodles' mouth.

Doodles didn't want the sandwich and he didn't want Milo's juice, either.

"Maybe you're not well," said Milo anxiously.

"Maybe I'm just not hungry," barked Doodles.

When it was Bella's turn to look after Doodles, she said she'd take him for a walk. Doodles raced to the door, barking loudly and wagging his tail.

"WAIT!" ordered Bella. "First you have to get dressed."

"But dogs don't wear clothes!" whined Doodles. Bella rummaged through the dressing-up box. "It's a nice sunny day," she said. "This shirt will be cool."

"Sunglasses will keep the sun out of your eyes."

"And a hat will stop your head from burning." At last Doodles was ready for his walk.

Milo followed Bella and Doodles into the garden.

"Doodles hasn't eaten his sandwich," he complained.

"Dogs don't eat sandwiches," said Bella. "They eat meat and bones."

"Where does Doodles keep his bones?" asked Milo.

"Dogs bury their bones," said Bella. "Where do you bury your bones, Doodles?"

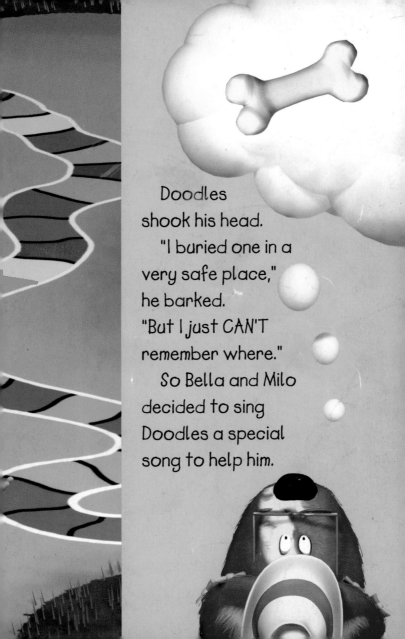

Doodles
shook his head.
"I buried one in a
very safe place,"
he barked.
"But I just CAN'T
remember where."
So Bella and Milo
decided to sing
Doodles a special
song to help him.

Where has Doodles buried his bone?

Ask that bee by the honeycomb!

Do you know where it can be?

Doodles's bone? Don't ask me. I've got honey for my tea.

Don't want honey. I want a bone! Doodles wants a BONE!

Where has Doodles buried
his bone?

Ask that cow there,
all alone.

Do you know where
it can be?

Doodles's bone?
Don't ask me.
I've got grass
for my tea!

Don't eat grass.
I want a bone.
Doodles wants a BONE!

Where has Doodles buried his bone?

Ask that bird. She's flown and flown.

Do you know where it can be?

Doodles's bone?
Don't ask me!
I've got worms
for my tea!

Don't want worms!
I want a bone!
Doodles wants a BONE!

The bone song made Doodles remember exactly where he'd buried his bone.

He kept on digging

and digging

and digging

until he found it.

"Clever boy, Doodles," said Bella.

Then Doodles heard someone calling him. "Doodles, Doodles!" Doodles pricked up his ears.

It was Jake and he scampered indoors.

Jake laughed when he saw Doodles.
"You look funny!" he teased.

Doodles barked and chased Jake, and
they rolled together all over the floor.

Off came the hat,

the sunglasses,

the ribbons,

the clothes,
the nappy...

"STOP THAT!"
yelled Fizz.

Bella and Fizz went to find Judy.

"Jake's messed up Doodles," they told her.

"I didn't mean to," cried Jake. "I was only playing with him. Anyway, Doodles looked silly in clothes!"

"No, he didn't!" said Bella. "He looked beautiful. And he was cool and dry and clean and everything."

"Jake's right," said Judy. "Dogs don't need to wear clothes. Doodles isn't like you or me. Doodles is a dog. He needs to be looked after just like a dog."

"What special things does Doodles need?" asked Fizz.

"Sandwiches?" asked Milo.

"Dogs need long walks, big bones, water, dog food and lots of love," said Judy.

"And dogs like to play," added Jake.

"Woof!" barked Doodles.
"That's what I like BEST!"

THE END